Row, Row, Row Your Boat

and

Ride, Ride, Ride Your Bike

D0320625

Notes for adults

TADPOLES ACTION RHYMES provide support for newly independent readers and can also be used by adults for sharing with young children.

The language of action rhymes is often already familiar to an emergent reader and the accompanying actions reinforce the narrative experience.

The alternative rhymes extend this reading experience further, and encourage children to play with language and try out their own rhymes and actions.

If you are reading this book with a child, here are a few suggestions:

1. Make reading fun! Choose a time to read when you and the child are relaxed and have time to share the story.
2. Recite the rhyme together before you start reading. What might the alternative rhyme be about? Why might the child like it?
3. Encourage the child to reread the rhyme and do the actions, and to retell it in their own words, using the illustrations to remind them what has happened.
4. Point out together the rhyming words when the whole rhymes are repeated on pages 12 and 22 (developing phonological awareness will help with decoding) and encourage the child to make up their own new rhymes.
5. Give praise! Remember that small mistakes need not always be corrected.

First published in 2010 by
Franklin Watts
338 Euston Road
London NW1 3BH

Franklin Watts Australia
Level 17/207 Kent Street
Sydney NSW 2000

Text (Ride, Ride, Ride Your Bike)
© Wes Magee 2010
Illustration © Marina Le Ray 2010

The rights of Wes Magee to be identified as
the author of Ride, Ride, Ride Your Bike
and Marina Le Ray as the illustrator of this
Work have been asserted in accordance
with the Copyright, Designs and Patents
Act, 1988.

ISBN 978 0 7496 9369 5 (hbk)
ISBN 978 0 7496 9375 6 (pbk)

Series Editor: Melanie Palmer
Series Advisors: Dr Hilary Minns
and Catherine Glavina
Series Designer: Peter Scoulding

Printed in China

Franklin Watts is a division of
Hachette Children's Books
an Hachette Livre UK company.
www.hachettelivre.co.uk

Row, Row, Row Your Boat

Retold by Wes Magee

Illustrated by Marina Le Ray

FRANKLIN WATTS

LONDON•SYDNEY

**Marina
Le Ray**

"I like the idea
of rowing a boat down
a stream on a lovely,
sunny day, and all the
wildlife you would see
along the way."

Row, row, row your boat

gently down
the stream.

Merrily, merrily,

merrily, merrily,

life is but a dream.

Row, Row, Row Your Boat

Row, row, row your boat

gently down the stream.

Merrily, merrily,

merrily, merrily,

life is but a dream.

Can you point to the
rhyming words?

Ride, Ride, Ride Your Bike

by Wes Magee
Illustrated by Marina Le Ray

Wes Magee

"The first time I tried to ride my new bike, I went too fast down the lane and I fell off!"

Ride, ride, ride your bike

up the muddy lane.

Bumpity, bumpity,
bumpity, bumpity,

ride it back again.

Ride, Ride, Ride Your Bike

Ride, ride, ride your bike

up the muddy lane.

Bumpity, bumpity,

bumpity, bumpity,

ride it back again.

Can you point to the
rhyming words?

Puzzle Time!

1.

2.

3.

Choose the right action
for the picture.

Answers

The correct action
is picture 3.